TABLE OF CONTENTS

CHAPTER 1
A SPECIAL INVITATION 5

CHAPTER 2
LATE? 14

CHAPTER 3
AN EMPTY SEAT 21

CHAPTER 4
A MAN IN A STORM 26

CHAPTER 5
THE DUSTY ROOM 34

CHAPTER 6
GENEROUS HOST 40

CHAPTER 7
THE END? 45

CHAPTER 8
SEEING IN THE DARK 50

CHAPTER 9
GIFTS 58

JASON STRANGE

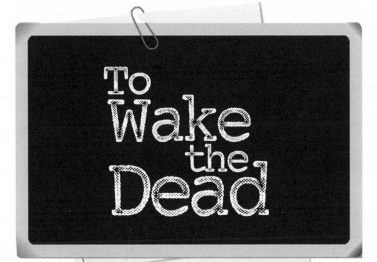

To Wake the Dead

Cover Illustration by Serg Soleiman

Interior Illustration by Phil Parks

STONE ARCH BOOKS
a capstone imprint

Jason Strange is published by Stone Arch Books
A Capstone Imprint
1710 Roe Crest Drive
North Mankato, Minnesota 56003
www.capstonepub.com

Copyright © 2011 by Stone Arch Books

Library of Congress Cataloging-in-Publication Data is available on the Library of Congress website.

Library Binding: 978-1-4342-2963-2
Paperback: 978-1-4342-3094-2

Summary: Grant receives an invitation to see a great classic horror movie. But real life is just as creepy as the film . . .

Art Director/Graphic Designer: Kay Fraser
Production Specialist: Michelle Biedscheid

Photo credits:
Shutterstock: Nikita Rogul (handcuffs, p. 2); Stephen Mulcahey (police badge, p. 2); B&T Media Group (blank badge, p. 2); Picsfive (coffee stain, pp. 2, 5, 12, 17, 24, 30, 42, 48, 57); Andy Dean Photography (paper, pen, coffee, pp. 2, 66); osov (blank notes, p. 1); Thomas M Perkins (folder with blank paper, pp. 66, 67); M.E. Mulder (black electrical tape, pp. 69, 70, 71)

Printed in China
062016   009835R

– Chapter 1: **A Special Invitation** –

Grant Gardner clenched his teeth so that he wouldn't yawn. He couldn't let his mother know how tired he was. When he couldn't fight it anymore, he turned to the car window and let the yawn come out.

His mom didn't notice. "Really, Grant," she said. "Why did I ever agree to this?"

Grant rolled his eyes. He continued staring out onto the dark streets of downtown as his mom's car crossed River Street.

"What other mother would let her thirteen-year-old son go to a midnight movie?" his mom went on. "And a horror movie, no less!"

"Come on, Mom," Grant said. He sighed. "We made a deal."

"I know, I know," his mom said. "I didn't think you'd keep up your end of the bargain, I guess."

Grant had kept up his end of the bargain.

It all started three months ago, when he got a strange, old-looking envelope in the mail one day. The letter was on his bed when he got home from school.

Grant wasn't used to getting mail, so he was excited about it. Still, the envelope looked very fancy, so he opened it slowly and carefully.

Inside was a single piece of paper — more like a card, really.

An invitation to a horror movie.

This invitation entitles the bearer to
a seat during a very special midnight
viewing of the classic thrilling horror film
THE GHOST OF MYSTIC MANOR
at the Riverview Downtown Theater.

There was no return address, and no signature. Besides the date of the showing and the address of the theater, there was no other information at all.

At first Grant couldn't imagine why he'd get such a cool invitation.

Then he realized. He was a member of about a hundred online horror fan communities. He subscribed to *Monsters and Mummies* magazine. He was even a member of the Horror Book of the Month Club.

Of course. That's why he'd gotten the invitation. He was probably on every single horror mailing list.

Grant had heard of *The Ghost of Mystic Manor*. It was a classic. But he'd never had the chance to see it. The movie hadn't ever come out on DVD, and theaters never showed it. He couldn't miss this chance.

Right away, Grant made a deal with his mom. He agreed to double his chores, even doing the laundry every week and cooking dinner twice a week. He also promised to keep all his grades at B or better — even in math class.

In return, Mom would bring him to the movie and pick him up afterward.

Somehow, Grant had done it. And the night was finally here.

They came to a red light near the bridge over the river. Grant's mom reached into her purse.

"Here," she said. She pulled out a single bill. "Twenty dollars. You can get some popcorn and a soda."

"Thanks," Grant said.

"I don't suppose I'll get any change?" she said as the light turned green. The car started moving again, into a dark, empty part of downtown.

"From twenty dollars?" Grant replied. He laughed. "I doubt it. Movie snacks are pretty expensive."

Mom shook her head. "It's shocking what these ghouls get away with nowadays," she said. "When I was a kid, twenty bucks would pay for me and all my friends to see a movie and get popcorn. And I'd still have some change."

"I know, I know," Grant said, rolling his eyes.

Mom's car pulled up to the theater.

The Riverview was the oldest theater in town. In fact, Grant's dad had been surprised that the movie was playing there. When Grant told him about the special showing, Dad said he'd thought that the Riverview Theater had closed down decades ago.

"Wow. They've certainly done a nice job of fixing the old place up," Grant's mom said, peering out at the building.

Grant nodded. It was a big, beautiful old theater.

"Yeah," he said. "Usually these buildings get bulldozed to make room for those big stadium theaters. I don't know. I think this is way cooler."

The theater's marquee hung out over the sidewalk, flashing with hundreds of light bulbs. In big black letters, the sign read *THE GHOST OF MYSTIC MANOR.*

The lights were all on out front, including over the small ticket booth. The booth stood alone on the sidewalk, in front of the big golden doors to the lobby. From the car, Grant could see that it was empty.

In fact, not a single person was anywhere to be seen. Most of the block — in fact, most of downtown Ravens Pass — was dark.

No other movie customers were lined up to get in, or chatting in the chilly night air about how excited they were. There were no big horror fans talking about the classic thrillers or the latest slashers.

The street was completely empty.

– Chapter 2: **Late?** –

"Must not be a very popular movie," Grant's mother said.

Grant glanced at his watch. It was already 11:59.

"I bet everyone else got here early," he said. "You know, to get popcorn or soda or whatever. Plus they probably didn't have to wait for a ride from their moms."

His mom rolled her eyes at him.

Grant laughed. "They're all probably already seated," he said. "I better hurry, huh?"

But his mom suddenly had a very serious look on her face. "Hmm," she said.

Grant swallowed. He knew what that look meant. It meant his mom was thinking twice about letting him go to the movie after all. Even after he'd worked his butt off for months.

"And that ticket booth," his mom went on. "It looks empty. Isn't anyone working here?"

"Um," Grant said. He tried to think fast. "They're probably collecting the invitations inside. It's a special showing, remember?"

"I don't know," his mom said. "This all seems a little weird to me."

"Mom," Grant whined. "It's fine."

Grant's mom twisted up her mouth. Then she pushed the button to open the window. "Hello?" she shouted out toward the theater.

"Stop!" Grant pleaded. "You're embarrassing me."

"Oh, please," his mom replied. Then she honked the car horn.

Grant jumped at the sound. Then he reached across to pull her hands from the wheel. "Mom!" he shouted. "Come on."

"I don't know about this, Grant," she said, shaking her head. "Why didn't anyone come outside? That horn honking was loud enough to wake the dead."

"No kidding," Grant muttered.

Then Grant had an idea.

"Wait a minute," he said. "I think I just saw someone get into the ticket booth."

"Really?" Mom said, leaning forward to see.

Grant opened his door and jumped out of the car. Then he ran to the ticket booth. "Hi!" he shouted. Of course, no one was actually there, but he wasn't going to let this night slip away from him.

"Here's my invitation," he said, waving the letter.

Then Grant noticed something. There was a little white box sitting on the counter, blocking the little hole in the glass that normally would be used to pass tickets through. On the box was a small slot, and there was a little sign on the window that read, "Insert tickets here."

Grant thought that was a little odd. First, an empty street and no other movie fans around. Now just a box to collect the tickets No one was even there.

But Grant didn't want to give up. Not after three months of extra chores and hours of homework every night.

His mom was watching, and if she thought things were weird she'd probably throw him back into the car and take him right home. No way. That wasn't going to happen.

Grant forced a smile and slipped his ticket into the box.

"Thank you," he said into the ticket booth, still faking it for his mom's sake. Then he turned to the car and gave her a big thumbs-up.

"Okay," Grant's mom shouted back through the open window. "I'll be back in exactly an hour and forty minutes! Come right out after the movie!"

"I know," Grant replied as he pulled open the big theater doors. "I'll be here." Then he went inside.

~ Chapter 3: **An Empty Seat** ~

When Grant walked in, the lobby was empty. It was bright, and very clean, and the glass counters were stocked well with popcorn and candies. There were several sofas and fancy-looking chairs, too.

The room was huge! The whole place was carpeted in red with tiny gold stars. Giant mirrors lined the wide columns that went up to the super-high ceiling. A gigantic, glittering chandelier hung from the ceiling.

But there was no one around — not an usher, not a customer, not even one single soul.

Grant stood for a moment near the front doors, taking it all in. He cleared his throat in the silence, and the sound echoed like he was in the Grand Canyon.

The smell of popcorn was everywhere. Grant walked over to the snack counter.

"Hello?" he said. But no one was there. Not even someone to sell snacks.

Grant didn't have time to buy anything anyway. The clock hanging behind the counter showed it was already two minutes after midnight.

He moved quickly through the big lobby right to the big swinging black doors, which led into the theater itself.

"I must really be the last person here," Grant muttered.

He stepped into the theater just as the movie's title appeared on the big screen.

The theater was pitch black. He couldn't even see the seats. Huge white creepy letters shined down on him, but that wasn't enough light to see by.

Grant stood by the door, hoping his eyes would get used to the dark.

"Hey," a voice whispered near him. "There's an empty seat right here, next to me."

Grant squinted into the darkness. Just a few feet away, he spotted something in the shadows, only a few rows from the back. The aisle seat was empty. Grant walked over and slid into the seat.

"Thanks," he said softly. "I was afraid I'd be standing there in the dark like a dork for ages."

His new neighbor laughed. Grant could tell it must be a girl, about his age.

He turned to the screen. The shot was moving slowly up a great long driveway, right toward the Mystic Manor itself.

Suddenly, lightning struck on the screen, lighting up the whole theater. Grant's heart thudded against his chest as he looked around.

The theater was completely empty. Only he and the girl next to him were there.

– Chapter 4: **A Man in a Storm** –

"We're the only ones here?" Grant asked, still whispering.

The girl replied, "Yes. You don't have to whisper, I guess."

"I guess not," Grant said. His voice sounded odd in the big empty theater, with the sound of thunder and rain in the movie.

"The opening credits are pretty long," the girl said. "I'll go get us some popcorn and sodas. Okay?"

"Oh, I can do it," Grant said, getting up. He stopped. "Wait, there was no one at the counter."

The girl got up too and moved past him. "That's okay," she said. "I, um, know the theater owners. They'll give me a discount. I'll be right back."

Grant sat back down and watched the credits. Most of them were more shots of the manor and the car going up the driveway. The rain was terrible, and every so often thunder would clap and lightning would flash across the landscape.

Each time lightning struck, Grant saw the big empty theater in front of him. A chill ran across his shoulders.

On screen, the car stopped at the top of the driveway. A tall man got out.

He was wearing a long coat, and he pulled it over his head to protect himself from the downpour. He hurried to the manor's front door and raised the heavy knocker.

Thud. Thud. Thud.

No one answered. He knocked again.

Thud. Thud. Thud.

Still, no one opened the door. The man no longer bothered covering his head with his coat. It wasn't helping at all. He was soaking wet.

"Hello?" he shouted over the storm, knocking again.

Thud. Thud. Thud.

"Please!" he shouted. "Some shelter from this storm!"

The man sighed. "This is madness," he mumbled to himself. "I've shouted and knocked loud enough to wake the dead."

"I'm back." Grant jumped at the girl's voice. She handed him a big cup of soda and sat down. Then she put a huge bucket of popcorn between them.

"Thanks," Grant said. He took a few pieces of popcorn and threw them into his mouth. They were hot and fresh, covered in butter. This popcorn was way better than any other movie theater popcorn he'd ever had.

"Wow," he said. "This is great popcorn."

"Thanks," the girl replied. "I popped it myself. I even melted the butter for it." She took a handful too and popped it into her mouth.

"Cool," Grant said. When he reached into the bucket for some more popcorn, their hands bumped.

"Oh, sorry," he said, feeling his face turn hot. The girl just giggled.

Lightning struck in the movie several times, and Grant tried to sneak glances at his neighbor's face. She was definitely around his age, but he didn't recognize her from school.

But how could that be? he thought. *There is no other public school around here. She must go to a private school or something.*

"Hey," Grant said as he took a handful of popcorn. "I'm Grant. What's your name?"

"I'm Ruthie," the girl replied. She reached for some popcorn and stuffed it into her mouth.

"So, how come I've never seen you before?" Grant asked. "Do you go to Franklin Middle School?"

"Um," the girl said. She looked at her hands, then at the movie. "Right, Franklin Middle School. Of course."

"Well, it is a big school," Grant replied. "I guess we just never had a class together."

Ruthie laughed. "That's probably it," she said. "Anyway, I'm glad you came to the movie tonight, Grant. It's too bad no one else did." She kept her eyes on the screen. "This is a classic," she said. "It's been my favorite movie since the day it opened."

Grant squinted at her face to see if she was kidding. He opened his mouth to remind her that this movie came out in the 1930s, long before even their parents were alive.

But just then she tilted her head toward him and pointed at the screen.

"The stranger is going into the manor," she said, leaning forward. Even in the dark Grant could tell that her face lit up as she spoke. She was so excited.

Grant decided to let it go. He leaned back, smiling, and watched the movie.

– Chapter 5: **The Dusty Room** –

Grant was loving the movie. It probably helped that his new friend Ruthie was such a big fan of *The Ghost of Mystic Manor*. Watching the movie with someone who loved it only made him love it more.

In the middle of the movie, the tall man was wandering through the manor. A young, beautiful woman had let him inside Mystic Manor, but now she was nowhere to be seen. He decided to poke around.

Grant and Ruthie watched the man climb a winding set of steps up to the second floor.

"I wouldn't go up there," Grant whispered. Ruthie laughed.

The man reached the top of the steps and found a long hallway. At the end of the hall was a big, fancy door. It stood open just slightly. He pushed it and it swung open.

The room was an old, dusty bedroom. It was full of furniture, most of it covered in dusty white sheets. Overhead was an old chandelier of candles, unlit. In the middle of the room was a huge wooden bed, with four posts and a ripped canopy made of dark fabric.

"The poor woman must live in this house all alone," the man muttered to himself. "I wonder how many unused rooms there are."

Ruthie nodded. "She must be lonely," she said quietly.

Suddenly, in the movie, footsteps approached from the hall. The tall man didn't want to be caught creeping and snooping around. He hurried from the room and pulled the door closed behind him.

When his host appeared, carrying a tall, bright candle, he smiled at her.

"Hello," the man said.

His host smiled back at him. "Are you lost?" she said kindly. "I thought we might enjoy a drink by the fire in the sitting room."

"That would be nice," the man replied. "I was just looking around. It's a lovely house."

"Thank you," his host said. She walked past him and pushed open the door he had closed. "Now how did this door get closed?"

She walked into the old bedroom. She held the candle before her. "If you'd like to spend the night, until this terrible storm passes," the woman said, "this will be your bedroom."

The man followed her in. "Oh, no," he said, seeming a little shocked that she'd put him in this dusty, crowded bedroom. "I don't want to bother you."

The room was brighter than it had been, thanks to the light coming from the woman's candle. The man gasped at the sight, and in his movie theater seat, so did Grant.

The room wasn't dusty or cluttered. In fact, it was amazing. The windows were big and clean. The furniture was uncovered. The bed looked perfect, covered with soft pillows and blankets, and the wooden posts looked like they'd been polished that day.

"Wow," the man said. "How . . . um, how do you keep the place so clean?"

The woman smiled at him. "You're too kind," she said.

Grant leaned closer to Ruthie and whispered, "How did she do that?"

"We have a lot of tricks up our sleeves," she said.

Grant laughed. "Girls do, you mean?" he said, and Ruthie giggled.

– Chapter 6: **Generous Host** –

Toward the end of the movie, the tall man was sitting in a big chair near a roaring fire. Across from him sat the young woman, his host. She was pale and fragile-looking, but very beautiful.

Still, something about the woman, in her old-fashioned dress, gave Grant the creeps.

"I love this part," Ruthie said. "This is where the man realizes he can never leave the haunted house."

Grant looked at Ruthie out of the corner of his eye. She was beaming at the screen now. Grant watched the movie.

The tall man sipped a drink from a fancy glass. It seemed to warm him up. His host leaned toward him, smiling.

"Can I get anything else for you?" she asked eagerly. "Would you like something to eat? You must be so hungry, driving all night."

The man smiled back. "That would be nice," he said. The woman leaned forward and took his hand. He immediately pulled it away.

"Your hand," the man said, his smile fading. "It's so cold."

The woman looked embarrassed. She turned away.

"Please," the man said. "Take the seat by the fire. You must warm up. I am dry now, and quite comfortable. Please."

The woman shook her head. "I'm always a little chilly," she said. "You stay in your seat. I'll be back with some tea cakes and finger sandwiches. It's no trouble."

The man got up, but his host had run off toward the kitchen.

"She's so kind," Ruthie said quietly. "She welcomes the stranger into her home and takes care of him."

Grant thought about it. "I guess so," he said. "But I have to admit, I think she's up to something."

Ruthie turned to face him. Her smile was gone. "That's awful," she said. "She simply wants some company. She's alone so often."

Grant felt terrible. This was the first time, it seemed, that Ruthie wasn't smiling since he'd sat down next to her. "I guess you're right," he said.

Ruthie began to smile again. Then she turned back toward the screen.

— Chapter 7: **The End?** —

Before long, the tub of popcorn between Grant and Ruthie was empty. Grant sucked at the straw of his soda, but it only made a loud slurping sound. He shook his cup. Empty.

"Would you like another soda, Grant?" Ruthie said. She started to get up.

"Oh, no," Grant said, a little startled. "I'm okay."

Ruthie sat back down. As she did, the movie screen suddenly turned a blinding white, then black.

The theater was pitch dark, and Grant could hear the film reel slapping on the projector from the booth above them.

"What happened?" Grant said. "The movie isn't over yet."

Ruthie yawned. "The print ripped," she said. Her smile was gone. She took a long sip through the straw of her soda.

"Do you think they'll fix it?" Grant asked.

Ruthie shook her head. "No," she said. "It's no big deal."

Grant was stunned. "But this is your favorite movie," he said. "Don't you want to see the end?"

"I never much liked the ending anyway," Ruthie said. "That awful man leaves the woman all alone in that big house. It's heartbreaking."

"So he escapes?" Grant asked.

"Escapes?" Ruthie repeated angrily. "He doesn't escape. He abandons her. After all she did for him. Taking him from the storm, feeding him, and giving him someplace to dry off. After being given so much, how can he just leave her there? She's all alone! It's awful."

"I don't get it," Grant said. "Isn't she . . . you know. The bad guy?"

Ruthie just laughed and sipped at her soda. "The movie is much better, ending this way. I gave the woman back her happy ending."

"What do you mean?" Grant asked. "I thought you said the film ripped, or something."

Ruthie shook her head. "Never mind," she said mysteriously.

– Chapter 8: **Seeing in the Dark** –

Grant squinted at his watch, but it was too dark to see the time. "Um, my mom is supposed to pick me up soon. I think," he said.

"Here," Ruthie said. She pulled something out of her pocket and clicked it on. A narrow beam of light shined onto Grant's wrist. It was already after 1:30 in the morning.

"Uh-oh," he said. "She'll be outside any second. I guess I better get out there."

In the light of Ruthie's penlight, Grant could just make out her face. She was very pretty, but her eyes were so tired and dark, and the rest of her face so pale.

"I guess we're not used to being up this late," Grant said. "You sure look tired."

Ruthie gasped and quickly switched off the light.

"Can't you leave that on?" Grant said. "I can't even see enough to find the door."

"Oh, the batteries died, I think," Ruthie said.

"But I heard you click the switch," Grant said. *Why is she acting so weird all of a sudden?* he wondered.

"You're wrong," Ruthie replied. "Come on. I'll show you the way out."

Grant stood up and felt Ruthie's hand close over his. It was ice cold.

"Ruthie," Grant said. "Your hand . . ."

"This way," Ruthie said, leading him.

She pulled open the big black swinging door. The lights from the lobby forced Grant to squint and shade his eyes.

As Ruthie led Grant through the big lobby, always a step in front of him so he couldn't see her face, the lights began to flicker.

Just for an instant, every few seconds, the room would go dark. When it did, Grant rubbed his eyes. They were playing weird tricks on him.

Every few seconds, the bulbs in the chandelier above and the shining lights behind the candy counter flickered out.

In the dark, Grant could just make out things he didn't see when the lights were on. *I must be really tired*, he thought. The glass counters looked cracked and empty.

Then the lights clicked back on, just as suddenly.

Again, they flickered off. A heavy layer of dust lay on the chairs and sofas throughout the lobby. The carpeting and fabric on the furniture was torn.

Then the lights came back on, and the lobby was clean and beautiful.

Once more, the room was dark. Overhead, the chandelier was covered in cobwebs. The popcorn machine, which had looked so well cared for in the light, was cracked and broken. It obviously hadn't been used in decades or more.

The lights switched back on. Ruthie stopped at the front doors and turned to face Grant. She didn't look quite so tired and pale here in the bright lights of the lobby.

Grant felt his confusion slipping away as he gazed at her. She was so pretty, and fun, and made great popcorn. He couldn't wait to hang out with her more.

Ruthie smiled when she saw him relax. "Isn't it a beautiful theater?" she said. "You can stay a little longer. We'll have more popcorn."

"I really can't," Grant replied, even though he desperately wanted to say yes. "Maybe I'll see you around school, sometime, though?"

"I doubt it," Ruthie replied, her face turning sad.

"Oh, sure we will," Grant said. "We're friends now, right? We can have lunch together. You could come over sometimes. Are you in any after-school clubs?"

The lights flickered again, and Grant gasped. Ruthie's face went suddenly pale, and her eyes sunk deeply into her face. For the briefest moment, she was no longer a young, pretty girl.

– Chapter 9: **Gifts** –

Grant tugged away his hand and dashed to the door. It was locked.

The lights clicked back on. Ruthie stood staring at him, once again a thirteen-year-old girl. "What's wrong, Grant?" she asked sweetly. "Don't you want to stay here? It's a beautiful theater, and I'm so lonely."

"Please let me go," Grant said. "My mother will be outside. She'll be worried."

"But I can't let you leave, Grant," Ruthie said, taking a step toward him. "After the gifts I've given you, how can you just leave me here? I'm all alone!"

"Gifts?" Grant said. He pulled and pushed at the front door, but it wouldn't budge.

"The invitation to this showing, for one thing," Ruthie said.

"That was from you?" Grant asked. "But why?"

Ruthie moved closer to Grant. "Yes. I wanted a friend to come. To watch movies with me. Someone to give gifts to."

"What other gifts?" Grant asked.

"The popcorn, the soda," Ruthie told him. "If you stay, you can have all the snacks you want. We'll watch classic horror movies every day. Think of how great it could be."

"Please," Grant said. "I'll pay you back for the snacks, and for the movie."

Ruthie laughed. "I couldn't accept anything," she said. "It was my pleasure."

Grant dug into his pocket for the twenty-dollar bill his mother had given him.

"Here," he said. He grabbed Ruthie's hand and pried her fingers open. He pressed the bill into her hand, and her fingers closed around it.

Grant yanked his hand away. As he did, Grant heard the lock click. He pulled open the heavy door and ran out into the night and his mother's waiting car.

"You're late," his mom said as she pulled away from the curb. "By five minutes."

"Sorry," Grant said, gasping for breath. "There were problems with the projector."

His mom sighed as they drove through the quiet streets of downtown Ravens Pass. "Well, did you enjoy the movie?" she asked.

Grant took a deep breath. Should he tell her about Ruthie, the ghost girl? His mom would never believe it.

"I guess," he said. "But the popcorn was really expensive, and I'm not sure I liked the ending." He turned to look, to get one last glimpse of Ruthie, but though the lights blazed above the marquee, no one could be seen, not even the girl.

Case number: 78545

Date reported: April 14

Crime scene: Riverview Theater, downtown Ravens Pass

Local police: Yun Sing, rookie

Civilian witnesses: Grant Gardner, age 13

Disturbance: Officer Sing saw a kid leaving the theater at 2 a.m. He didn't question him.

Suspect information: This isn't the first time something strange has gone down at the Riverview. Back in 1985, a teenage boy went missing after seeing a movie there. His parents said he'd been to a special viewing, but the theatre's owners said the building had been closed. That case is still unsolved.

CASE NOTES:

I WAS CALLED IN AROUND NOON ON THE DAY AFTER OFFICER SING NOTED THE CIVILIAN WITNESS LEAVING THE SCENE. THOUGH HE HADN'T INTERVIEWED THE BOY, HE CALLED THE THEATER'S OWNERS, WHO REPORTED THAT POPCORN HAD BEEN MADE AND SOME CANDY HAD BEEN TAKEN FROM THE CONCESSION STAND.

IT SEEMED LIKE A TYPICAL BREAK-IN. BUT WHEN THEY LOOKED FURTHER, THEY FOUND AN OLD PRINT OF A CLASSIC HORROR MOVIE—A RARE ONE THEY HAD NEVER OWNED.

I INTERVIEWED THE CIVILIAN WITNESS, WHO TOLD ME THE WHOLE STORY. THEN I RECOMMENDED THAT THE BUILDING BE CLOSED PERMANENTLY. THE OWNERS SAID THEY MAY TRY TO FIGHT THE DECISION, BUT IN MY OPINION, WE CAN'T RISK LOSING MORE KIDS THERE. GRANT WAS LUCKY.

DEAR READER,

THEY ASKED ME TO WRITE ABOUT MYSELF. THE FIRST
THING YOU NEED TO KNOW IS THAT JASON STRANGE IS
NOT MY REAL NAME. IT'S A NAME I'VE TAKEN TO HIDE MY
TRUE IDENTITY AND PROTECT THE PEOPLE I CARE ABOUT.

YOU WOULDN'T BELIEVE THE THINGS I'VE SEEN, WHAT I'VE
WITNESSED. IF PEOPLE KNEW I WAS TELLING THESE STORIES,
SHARING THEM WITH THE WORLD, THEY'D TRY TO GET ME TO
STOP. BUT THESE STORIES NEED TO BE TOLD, AND I'M THE
ONLY ONE WHO CAN TELL THEM.

I CAN'T TELL YOU MANY DETAILS ABOUT MY LIFE. I CAN TELL
YOU I WAS BORN IN A SMALL TOWN AND LIVE IN ONE STILL. I
CAN TELL YOU I WAS A POLICE DETECTIVE HERE FOR TWENTY-
FIVE YEARS BEFORE I RETIRED. I CAN TELL YOU I'M STILL
OUT THERE EVERY DAY AND THAT CRAZY THINGS ARE STILL
HAPPENING.

I'LL LEAVE YOU WITH ONE QUESTION—IS ANY OF THIS TRUE?

JASON STRANGE
RAVENS PASS

Glossary

abandon (uh-BAN-dun)—leave alone

bargain (BAR-guhn)—a deal

chandelier (shan-duh-LEER)—a decorative light fixture with branches for several bulbs or candles

classic (KLASS-ik)—judged over time to be one of the best

ghouls (GOOLZ)—creepy people

manor (MAN-ur)—a large, stately home

marquee (mar-KEE)—a large awning or rooflike structure over a theater entrance

print (PRINT)—a copy of a motion picture on film

shelter (SHEL-tur)—protection

stocked (STOKD)—filled

DISCUSSION QUESTIONS

1. Who was Ruthie?

2. Should Grant tell his mom about the girl he met at the movie theater?

3. Grant loves horror movies. What's your favorite kind of movie? Why?

WRITING PROMPTS

1. Write a story about Ruthie before she became a ghost.

2. At the end of this book, Grant is heading home. What happens next? Use your imagination! Write a chapter that extends this book.

3. Pretend you're Ruthie. Write a diary entry about what happened in this book.

Weird
THINGS
Happen in
RAVENS
PASS.

JASON STRANGE

writes about them.

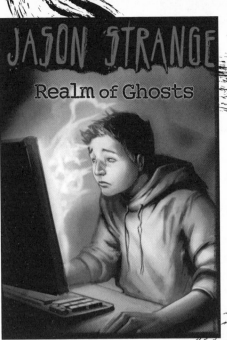

JASON STRANGE

Realm of Ghosts

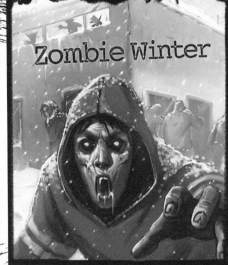

Zombie Winter

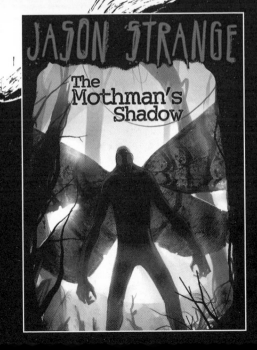

JASON STRANGE

The
Mothman's
Shadow